1971

The
Inner City
Mother
Goose

by Eve
Merriam

Visuals by
Lawrence
Ratzkin

Simon and
Schuster
New York

Text copyright ©
1969 by Eve Merriam;
Illustrations
copyright © 1969
by Lawrence Ratzkin.

FOURTH PRINTING
SBN 671-20289-8 Cl.
SBN 671-20290-1 Pa.
LC Number: 75-92194
Printed in the U.S.A.

Published by
Simon and Schuster,
Rockefeller Center,
630 Fifth Avenue,
New York, N.Y. 10020.

The Nub of The Nation

This is the nub of the nation:
In that nation is a city,
In that city is a ghetto,
In that ghetto is a street,
On that street there is a house,
In that house there is a stair,
On that stair there is a door,
Through that door there waits a room,
In that room there is a chair,
On that chair there is a person
Sitting staring there.

Sitting staring there
On the broken chair,
Chair in the cockroach room,
Room on the worn-out stair,
Stair in the no-care house,
House on the drop-dead street,
Street in the ghetto rot,
Ghetto rooted in the city,
City spreading everywhere:
And this is the nub of the nation.

Remembering Jesse B. Semple's daddy

Contents

Boys and Girls Come Out to Play

Boys and girls come out to play,
The moon doth shine as bright as day.
Leave your supper and leave your sleep,
And join your playfellows in the street.
Come with a whoop and come with a call:
Up, motherfuckers, against the wall.

Mary, Mary

Mary, Mary,
Urban Mary,
How does your sidewalk grow?

With chewing gum wads
And cigarette butts
And popsicle sticks
And potato chip bags
And candy wrappers
And beer cans
And broken bottles
And crusts of pizza
And coffee grounds
And burnt-out light bulbs
And a garbage
   strike all in a row.

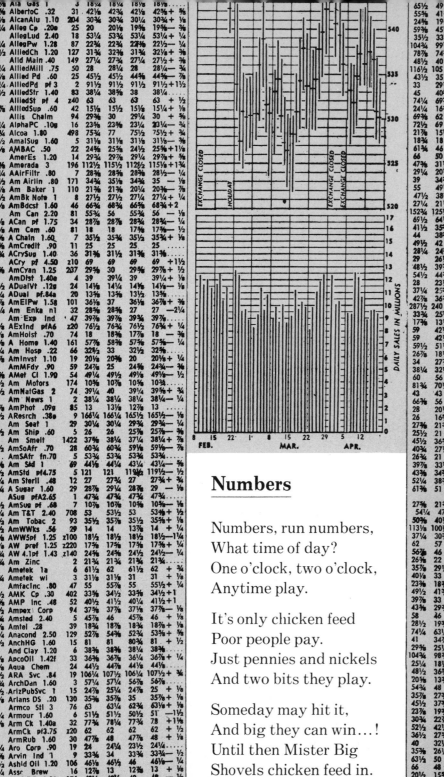

Numbers

Numbers, run numbers,
What time of day?
One o'clock, two o'clock,
Anytime play.

It's only chicken feed
Poor people pay.
Just pennies and nickels
And two bits they play.

Someday may hit it,
And big they can win…!
Until then Mister Big
Shovels chicken feed in.

There Was a Crooked Man

There was a crooked man,
And he did very well.

Tweedledum and Tweedledee

Tweedledum and Tweedledee
Agreed to disagree
And this was difficult you see
Because they shared so many views
And paid identical country club dues
And their children averaged the same I.Q.s
And not that they were prejudiced
There were charities they were glad to assist
And vocational scholarships they had backed
But neighborhood schools should be kept intact —

Just then rose up a great dark crowd
Crying out "Black Power!"
Which frightened both the heroes so
They outdid one another in vying for the honor of naming
the newly integrated neighborhood school
Malcolm X. Jefferson.

If Wishes Were Horses, Beggars Would Ride

If wishes were horses, beggars would ride,
And rich and poor in peace would abide.
If only the poor would smell sweet and be neat
And clean up the street

And talk nice and polite
And not publicly fight
And have college degrees
And station wagon keys
And interesting jobs that were also secure
— Or else kept out of sight and learned to endure —
There'd be nothing wrong with their just being poor

Take-a-Tour,
Take-a-Tour,
Congressman

Take-a-tour,
Take-a-tour,
Congressman,

Cover the ghetto
As fast as
You can:

Whisk through,
Tsk-tsk through,
And file under P:

Now you're
An expert
On Poverty.

Sing a Song of Subways

Sing a song of subways,
Never see the sun;
Four-and-twenty people
In room for one.

When the doors are opened —
Everybody run.

Black Youth, Black Youth

Black youth, black youth,
Have you any wool?

Yes, because
Black is beautiful and I'm letting
My hair grow full.

Here We Go Round

Here we go round the official list,
Official list,
Official list,
Here we go round the official list,
Official list again.

Welfare allowance for shoes this year,
Shoes this year,
Sign right here,
You're entitled to buy brand-new
Half a shoe this year.

Now I lay me down to sleep
I pray the double lock will keep;
May no brick through the window break,
And no one rob me till I wake.

Lucy Locket

Lucy Locket lost her pocket,
Kitty Fisher found it;
Not a penny was there in it,
Only ribbon round it.

                    Kitty got mad and cut Lucy up.

Taffy

Taffy is a storeman,
Taffy is a thief;
Taffy overcharges
For a tough piece of beef.

Taffy's cheese is moldy,
His eggs are sold with cracks;
There are seldom more than five
In his six-bottle packs.

His sacks of potatoes
Are sprouting with eyes;
There's hardly any fruit,
But many fruit flies.

His frozen food case
Has a constant leak;
His floor is never swept,
His milk is from last week.

Taffy's stock is low,
Yet somehow Taffy thrives:
Taffy offers credit
Till the monthly check arrives.

Prime Fres

$45.⁹⁰

14 OZ.

BELUG

58867

Jack Be Nimble
Jack Be Quick

Jack be nimble
Jack be quick

Snap the blade

And give it a flick

Grab the purse
It's easily done
Then just for kicks
Just for fun

Plunge the knife

And   cut

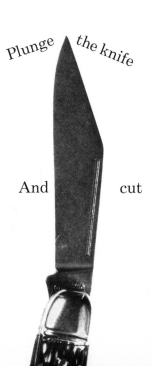

and run...

Simple Simon

$imple $imon
Met a high man
In the government.

$aid $imple $imon
To the high man,
"How are taxes spent?"

"Billions," said the high man,
"For an antimissile system
  That's bound
  To be obsolete
  Before it ever
  Gets off the ground."

"But that's ridiculous!"
  $aid $imple $imon.
"If people knew,
  They'd make a fuss."

"True," said the high man,
"And when you take into account
  That for just about half that amount
  Everybody could have a decent job
  And a house in a decent neighborhood."

"Fantastic," said $imple $imon,
"I don't believe it."

  $aid the high man,
"Good."

Pussy Cat,
Pussy Cat,
Where Have You Been?

Pussy cat,
Pussy cat,
Where have you been?

>To the City Hall hearing,
>But couldn't get in.

Pussy cat,
Pussy cat,
Why was that?

>It was all about cats
>And their habitats,
>But they only admitted
>Dogs and rats.

Fire

Fire! Fire! said Mrs. Dyer;

Where? Where? said Mrs. Dare;

In that part of town, said Mrs. Gown;

So no worry at all, said Mrs. Hall.

Only to them, said Mrs. Hem;

Any damage? said Mrs. Gamage;

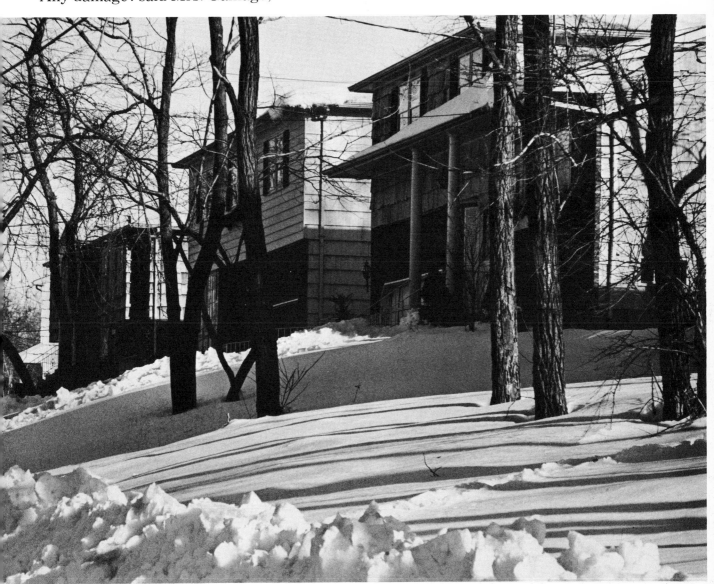

**Oh Where,
Oh Where Has
My Little Dog Gone?**

Oh where, oh where has my little dog gone?
Oh where, oh where can he be?

DOGS ALLOWED.
BALL PLAYING.
LOITERING.
PEDDLERS.
SOLICITING.
BICYCLING.
ROLLER SKATING.
ENTRANCE AFTER DARK.
EXIT.

THIS IS PUBLIC PROPERTY

Oh,
The Brave Old City of New York

Oh, the brave old city of New York
Took over ten thousand tenements
From absentee landlords who never made repairs
For any of the ghetto residents.

Now the tenements are there, are there,
And they're still not in repair, in repair;
But the residents now know who
Isn't making the repairs that are due.

Diddle Diddle Dumpling

Diddle diddle dumpling, my son Juan
Went to bed with his trousers on
And with the rest of the family
Sharing a single-room occupancy.

35

Hickety, Pickety,
My Black Hen

Hickety, pickety, my black hen,
Eggs for ladies and gentlemen,
Breakfast service graciously laid.
Gone with the wind: the sleep-in maid.

Wisdom

A wise old judge sat in a court,
The case was long, his judgment short;
Why change the way it's always been?
Convict the man of darker skin.

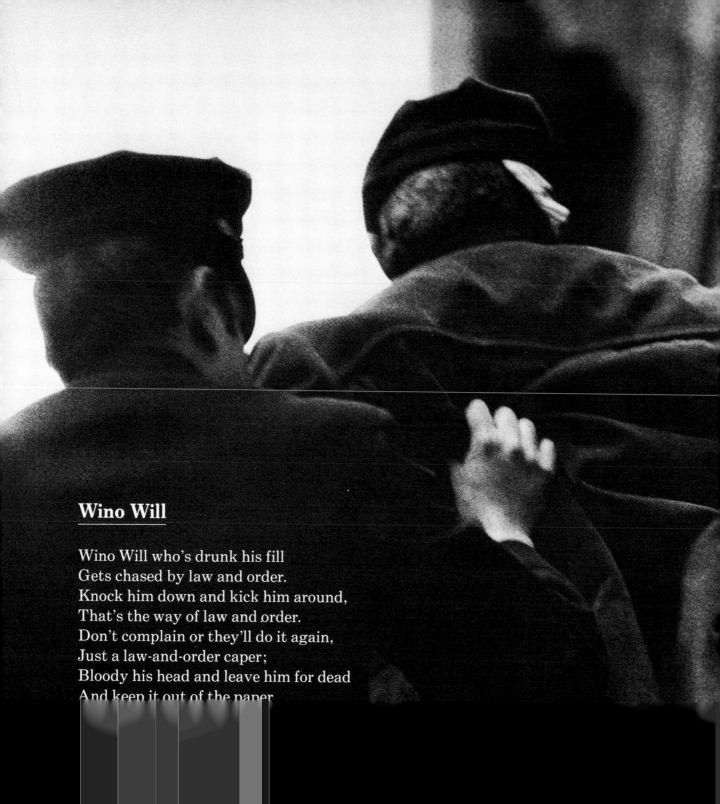

Wino Will

Wino Will who's drunk his fill
Gets chased by law and order.
Knock him down and kick him around,
That's the way of law and order.
Don't complain or they'll do it again,
Just a law-and-order caper;
Bloody his head and leave him for dead
And keep it out of the paper.

Poverty Program Hot, Poverty Program Cold

Poverty program hot,
Poverty program cold;
Poverty program cut
When a few months old.

The open door is shut,
The coffee pot's cold;
The Help Yourself leaflets
Are gathering mold.

Some write to protest:
Why did it fold?

Thank you for inquiring

Is all they are told.

Little Jack Horner

Little Jack Horner
Sat in the corner
Thumbing his first-grade book.

Look, Jack,
Look at blonde Jane and blue-eyed Dick
And their nice white house
And their nice green lawn
And their nice clean town
And their dog that is brown.

Little Jack Horner,
Dumb in the corner,
Why don't you learn to read?

Three Young Cats

Three young cats with Afro hats,
Robes with flowing angel wings,
Tiki pendants on leather strings,
Zulu beads and belts and rings
Went out to walk with three young girls
In natural wigs with nylon curls.

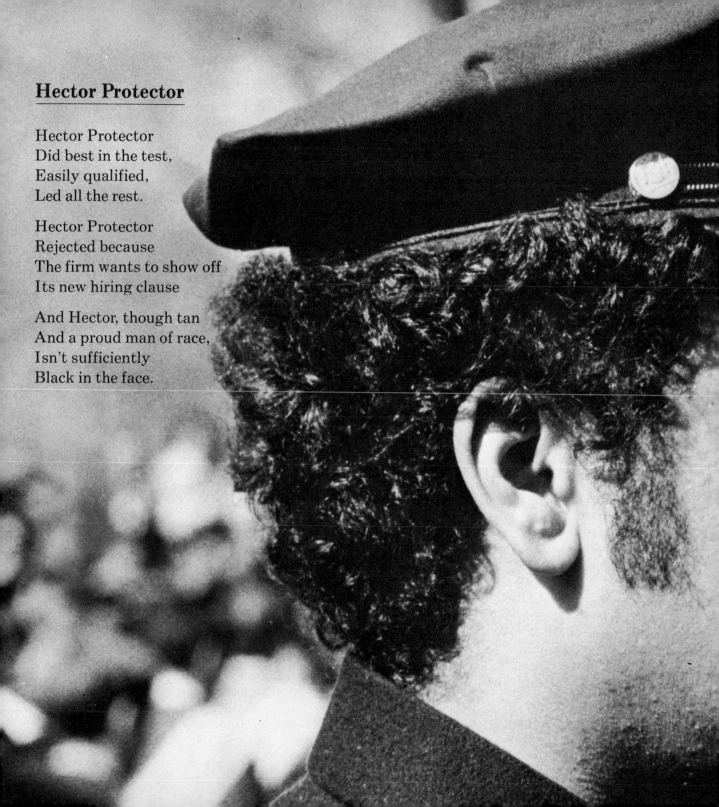

Hector Protector

Hector Protector
Did best in the test,
Easily qualified,
Led all the rest.

Hector Protector
Rejected because
The firm wants to show off
Its new hiring clause

And Hector, though tan
And a proud man of race,
Isn't sufficiently
Black in the face.

Christmas Is Coming

Christmas is coming,
The advertising's fat,
Please to put a dollar
In the old man's hat.
If you haven't got a dollar,
Then half will have to do;
If you haven't got a half a buck,
Then God mug you!

Star Light,
Star Bright

Star light,
Star bright,
Is it true the stars
Are clear at night?
Do they shine
Like traffic lights in lines,
Or do they glow
Like neon signs?
Do they hurt your eyes
Like the flashlight's glare
When you're told to halt
With your hands in the air?
Are they white as the clinic's
Overhead light?
Do they burn out at dawn?
Turn on every night?

Cherry Stones

Tinker,
Tailor,
Soldier,
Sailor,
Rich man,
Culturally disadvantaged underachiever.

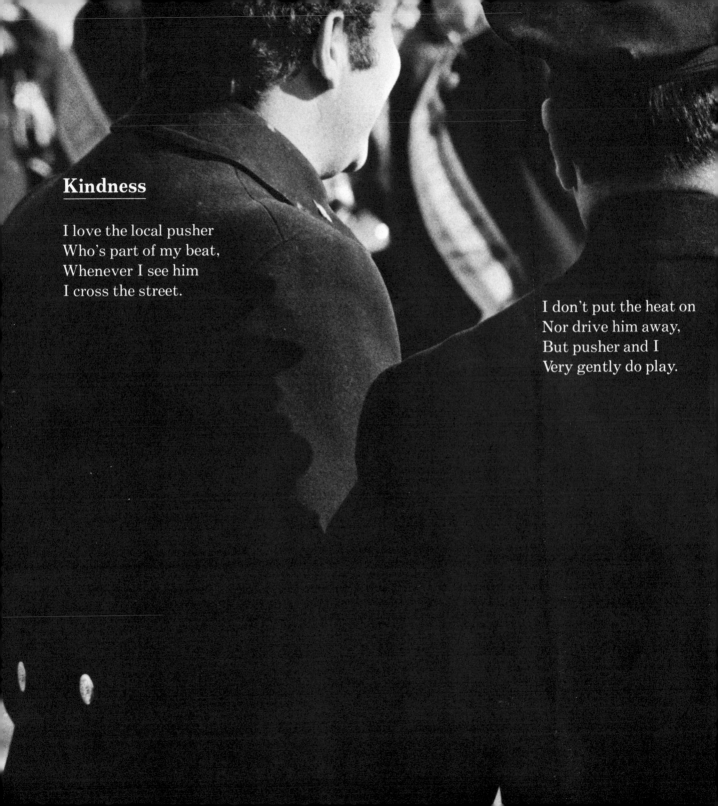

Kindness

I love the local pusher
Who's part of my beat,
Whenever I see him
I cross the street.

I don't put the heat on
Nor drive him away,
But pusher and I
Very gently do play.

I don't see a thing,
And I wish him good day;
Who can make ends meet
On just a cop's pay?

Ding, Dong, Bell

Ding, dong, bell,
The rat control is on the way,
The sweeper trucks are starting to spray,
The garbage trucks are beginning to hum,
The exterminator may even come!

They've got to disinfect it some,
For the mayor's coming to look today
At daily life in a slum.

You'll Find Mice

You'll find mice, see how they run!
They all ran out from behind the stove,
One climbed on the table and down he dove,
Then over the bread box he poked his head,
And back to his favorite spot once more,
To the bureau drawer that's set out on the floor
For baby's bed.

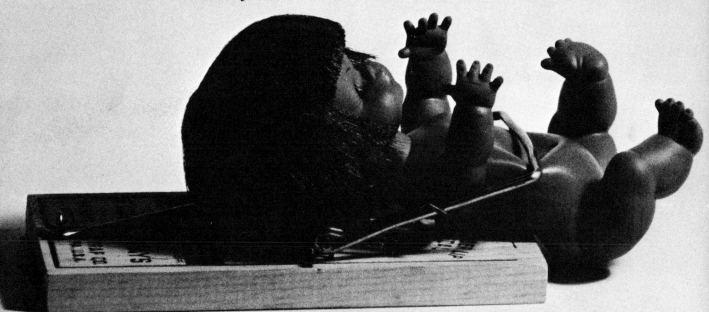

The Recruiting Sergeant

Come here to me, my merry merry men,
Said a sergeant loud and clear;

And the young men all were very merry men,
And they all came running near.
And the flag flew in the air,
And the drummer drummed his share,

And the sergeant spoke of Liberty
And pay and opportunity,
And the boys cried out

Hell no!
We won't go!

Robin and Richard

Robin and Richard,
Two young city men,
Lay in bed
Till the clock struck ten;
Then up starts Robin
And looks at the sky,
Oh, brother Richard,
The sun's very high.
No matter, says Richard,
What time it may be,
There are no jobs
For you or for me.

RICHARDSON-MERRELL INC.

22 East 42 St.
(opposite Grand Central)

An Equal Opportunity Employer
A member of Plans for Progress

SECRETARY

SOMETHING DIFFERENT?

THE CONFERENCE BOARD is a unique institution. Our staff conducts original research in the social sciences, government-business relations, and management. We publish books & magazines.

Our secretarial positions are also unique. Right now, we have a magazine editor, a researcher/writer, and a conference program administrator who need secretaries.

Average steno & typing skills needed for 2 positions; the other requires dictaphone exp.

STARTING SALARY: TO $125
TUITION AIDE
FREE BENEFITS

Contact: MISS SUSAN DORSET

NATIONAL INDUSTRIAL CONFERENCE BOARD

845 3rd Ave (51 St) PL 9-090 Ext 286

SECRETARY

For Young Executive
Infants Wear Firm

Good Skills Needed. Advancement.
Salary open. Brand new building

TERRY, LA 4-141

SECY $135 FEE PD

DURING THE SUMMER

Hrs: 9 to 4

Regular hrs. 9-4:45
12 Holidays
PLUS VACATION THIS YEAR
3 WEEKS NEXT YEAR
TERRIFIC BENEFITS

ACTION Agencies

175 Broadway   132 W 34th St.

SECYS   "FEE PAID" $6-8000

"WALL ST"

Prestige nat'l co offers divers stimulting spots in Jr & Sr ptnrs. Terrific ptnl & all bnfts pd & a 30% yr end bonus.

S-C-O-T-T

Mon. to Fri.
9 AM-5 PM

SECRETARIES   NO FEE

TEMPORARY

DAYS, WEEKS, MONTHS

$3.25

Per Hr.

For A Better Temporary Job

SWING TO DOT

Girls
Div of Dictaphone Corp

MIDTOWN   CHRYSLER BLDG 42 & LEX
DOWNTOWN 150 BROADWAY (nr. Wall)
BRONX   120 E. FORDHAM ROAD

817-3525

SECY!
GAL-MAN FRIDAY!
GOOD STENO NECESSARY

Major Midtown
New York City Firm
Seeks Right Hand for
Young Dynamic Group
of Research Engineers.

VARIETY OF DUTIES
INVOLVE CONFIDENTIAL
PRODUCTS, REPORTS
AND STATEMENTS.

FOR APPT. PLEASE CALL
KAY KOLNER
212-340-4486

SECRETARY
NBC

A position in our Legal Dept. is open for a well skilled secretary with at least 2 years experience. Apply 9 to 12:30, Monday thru Thursday, in Room 728; or send resume:

National Broadcasting Co.
30 Rockefeller Plaza (49-50 Sts.)
CI 7-830 , Ext 236.

An Equal Opportunity Employer

SECRETARY

TEMPORARY   NO FEE
EXECUTIVE   TRANSCRIPTION

TO $3.75/HR

MEDICAL   GENERAL   LEGAL
+ FRIDAY PAY + $ BONUS

PRO-TEMPS

130 W. 41 ST.   RM 652   594-4747

SECY JR. ADS $110 FEE PD

STATEN ISLAND: 40 Richmond Terrace

FOR L.I., WESTCHR, N.J. & CONN.
SEE LOCAL PHONE DIRECTORY

SECTY
TO
Regional & District
Sales Managers

Min 1-Yr Exp Plus Good Skills
5-Days, 9 AM-5 PM
$115-$125 WEEK
PLUS EXCELLENT BENEFITS

Good Advancement Oppty !

Call Mr Wal , 661-788
THE

HERTZ
CORPORATION
EAST SIDE AIRLINE TERMINAL
645 FIRST AVE (37 ST)
An equal opportunity employer

I Do Not Like Thee

I do not like thee,
applicant Fell;
The reason why I cannot tell
Because I'm

An equal opportunity employer.

SECRETARY

Non-profit educational organization, Africa related, seeks responsible, highly motivated secretary for on-the-job training program. General clerical duties, heavy telephone, may eventually handle own correspondence, and interview trainees and employes. Good typing and steno required, will also work from dictaphone. Stimulating fast paced office. Salary to $125, depending on prior earnings and experience. Liberal benefits.

Call Mr. Sade at 421-2500

African-American Institute
866 U. N. Plaza   N. Y. C
An Equal Opportunity Employer

SECRETARY-TYPING

LITE STENO
General Motors Benefits

APPLY IN PERSON

PONTIAC MOTOR DIVISION
GENERAL MOTORS BLDG
767 5th Ave, Room 406

An equal opportunity employer

SECYS   BIZ/HS/COLLEGE

LINE GRADS

Secretary

No Sten

You'll thoroughly enjoy working in our Budget Department. If figures! You'll be assisting bright, young Financial Analysts working on capital assets.

Knowledge of adding machine and a good phone personality are required.

The starting salary is $115 and the benefits including discounts on all Singer products are excellent.

INTERVIEWS DAILY until 4 PM.
PERSONNEL DEPT., 60th Fl.

SINGER

Diversified . Worldwide
30 Rockefeller Plaza, NYC

An Equal Opportunity Employer

Secretary

PUBLIC RELATIONS

P.R. division of Madison Avenue ad agency seeks brite secretary to work for account executive. Good skills required, experience preferred. Diversified duties, liberal benefits and friendly atmosphere.

Call Miss Cathy Albanese
421-4800 for appointment

SECRETARY
TO TRAFFIC MGR
GET ON THE MOVE!

Excellent skills + 1-2 yrs exp
Congenial atmosphere. Grand Cent. Area

HIGH SALARY
Liberal Co paid Benefits
Frequent salary reviews

hone   86-9512
An equal opportunity employer

SECRETARY

--NO PRESSURE--

in sales department
working with our salesmen.

--EASY TRAVEL--
ON BROADWAY- 242 ST LINE

Large air-cond offices, professional (chemical) firm in upper Manh w th a staff of over 30 women and 80 men.

FOundation 8-100 , Ext. 25

SECRETARIES $135-175 TO START

SHIPPING

Company has excellent opportu-

Excellent opportunity for brite & attractive Secty with 1-2 yrs exp and good skills to work in our Executive HQ on convenient midtown Madison Avenue.

5 Day, 35 Hour Week
Periodic Performance Review
Good Starting Salary
Good Company Benefits
Company Subsidized Cafeteria
Promotion from within Policy

APPLY IN PERSON, 9 AM-5PM
PERSONNEL DEPT., 9TH FLOOR
THE

HERTZ
CORP.
660 MADISON AVE. (61 ST)
an equal opportunity employer

SECRETARY-EXEC

TAKE YOUR CHOICE OF UNUSUALLY GOOD OPENINGS!

ALL FEE PAID!

Now that you are making a change why not pick the kind of company you want, the industry you want, and the kind of deal you prefer. All you need do is talk with our expert counselor Mr. Jenkins.
663-401

DUNHILL
Seventh Ave &   (Agency)

SECRETARY

TRAINEES

Lt steno or Speed-
writing essential
Diversified duties.
Publishing
Grand Central Area.

PHONE FOR APPOINTMENT
YU 6300, Ext 208

An Equal Opportunity Employer

SECYS   FEE PAID   TO $60

AIRLINES

AID DASHING YOUNG JET EXECS WITH THIS LEADING CARRIER. ENJOY HEAVY PUBLIC CONTACT. FREE WORLD TRAVEL. NEVER ANY FEE JOBS ALL FREE
(Agency) FOR SPECIAL AIRLINES CALL JIM KELLY SUNDAY OR COME IN EARLY MONDAY

GROWTH

147 W 42   (Phone 889-1960)   Rm 11

SFCY   FEE PAID $130 to $1

FOR THE SECRETARY WHO HATES THE THOUGHT OF BEING AVERAGE.

The average secy is doomed to a life of dull work, dull co-workers, surroundings, etc.

If

If all the seas were one sea,
What a *great* sea that would be!
If all the slums were one slum,
What a *great* slum that would be!
And if all the axes were one ax,
What a *great* ax that would be!
And if all the men were one man,
What a *great* man that would be!
And if the *great* man took the *great* ax,
And cut down the *great* slum,
And let it fall into the *great* sea —
What a *great* IF that would be!

Hey Diddle Diddle

Hey diddle diddle,
Hem haw and fiddle;
How do we integrate?

A jot and a tittle,
Too late and too little,
That's how we integrate.

Here am I,
Little Jumping Joan

Here am I,
Little Jumping Joan;
When nobody's with me
I'm all alone.

My daddy's gone,
And my mommy's gone till dark
Strolling with a carriage
In the park.

Lady's baby out
With my mommy all day,
While I stay in
By myself and play.

What Are Summer Nights Made Of?

What are summer nights made of, made of?
What are summer nights made of?

Too much heat,
Junk on the street,
Fire alarms,
Patrol cars,
Pickups and payoffs in bars.

What Are Winter Nights Made Of?

What are winter nights made of, made of?
What are winter nights made of?

Not enough heat,
Junk on the street,
Fire alarms,
Patrol cars,
Payoffs and pickups in bars.

HARK, HARK

THE DOGS DO

BARK

THE NEIGHBORS

YELL

THE BABIES

CRY

THE BUSES

GRIND,

THE TELEPHONES

THE BONGOS

RING,

BONG

THE JET PLANES

FLY,

HONK

THE CAR
HORNS

THE TAXIS **SCREECH,**
THE RADIO'S **ON, THE ROCK-**
THE TEEVEE'S **HIGH, AND-ROLL**
THE SUBWAY **ROARS** POURS FROM THE RECORD STORES, THE OLD WOMEN **MUTTER** ALONG THE GUTTER,
THE RATS **SQUEAK,**
THE FLIES **BUZZ:**

Only the roaches quietly crawl.

The Rule

Our school had a teaching staff,
Mostly white as snow,
And every time that tests were made,
The pupils rated low.

It happened that in every grade
Black children were the rule;
It made the parents good and mad
To see their local school.

And so in time it came about
That parents took control;
They turned the rule book teachers out
And hired those with soul.

And now the eager children learn,
To school they gladly go
With beaming teachers who are black
And some as white as snow.

Taxi Man

Taxi man, taxi man,
Quick drive me home!
My house is on fire
And my children all—!

Sorry, lady,
Even in an emergency
Cabs don't go to Harlem.

To Market

To market,
Supermarket,
To buy a full quart;

Home again,
Open it:
Measure is short.

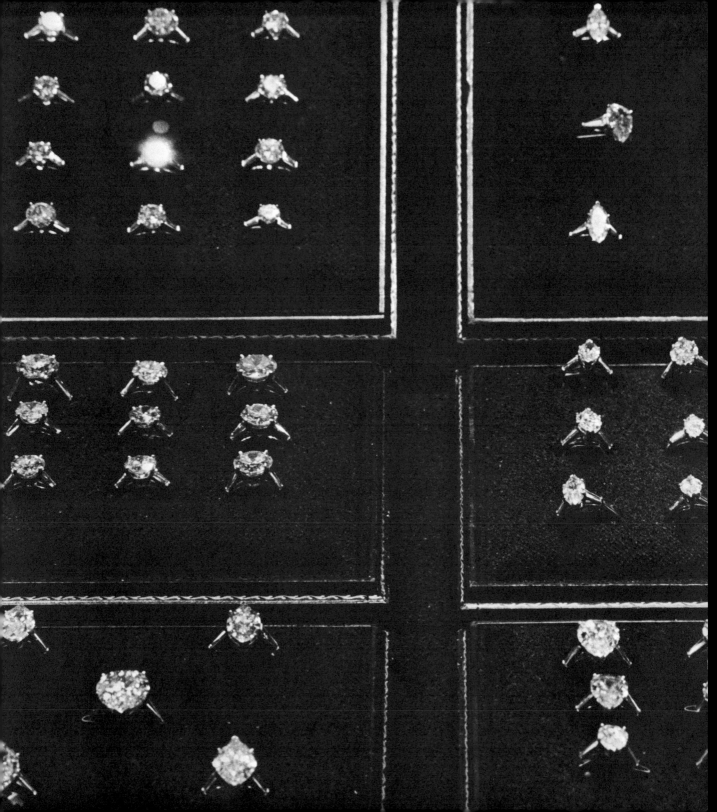

Bow-Wow, Says The Dog

Bow-wow, says the dog,

Mew, mew, says the cat,

Grunt, grunt, goes the hog,

And squeak, goes the rat.

Tu-whu, says the owl,

Caw, caw, says the crow,

Quack, quack, says the duck,

And what the Man says, you know.

Solomon Grundy

Solomon Grundy
Born on Slumday...

...this is the end
Of Solomon Grundy.

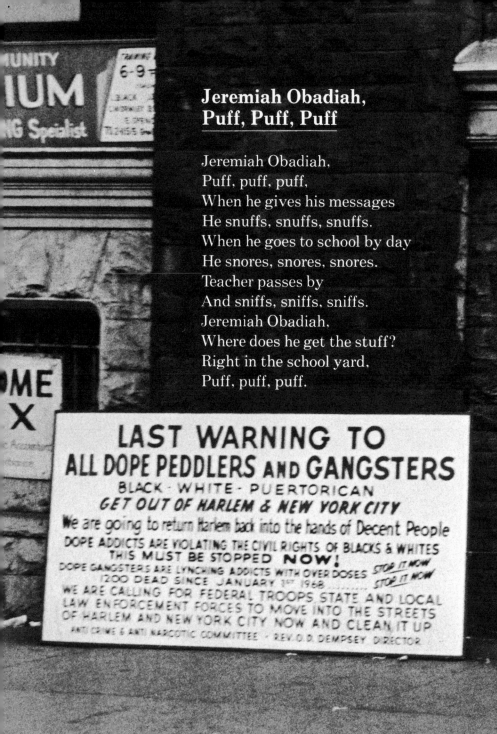

Jeremiah Obadiah, Puff, Puff, Puff

Jeremiah Obadiah,
Puff, puff, puff,
When he gives his messages
He snuffs, snuffs, snuffs.
When he goes to school by day
He snores, snores, snores.
Teacher passes by
And sniffs, sniffs, sniffs.
Jeremiah Obadiah,
Where does he get the stuff?
Right in the school yard,
Puff, puff, puff.

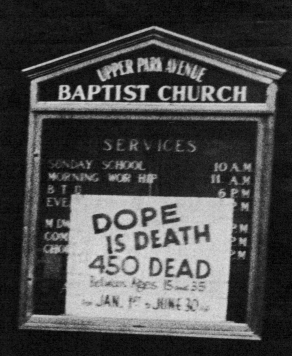

The Cow Jumped Over the Moon

The cow jumped over the moon
On the street in the afternoon;
The junkie laughed to see such sport
With his bag and his needle and spoon.

Rub-a-Dub-Dub

Rub-a-dub-dub,
Ceiling's in the tub;
And how do you think it got there?

Water in the tub
On the floor up above;
And that's how our ceiling got there.

On Teevee

On teevee
       see the looters run
With whiskey
        and cartons
            of cigarettes,
With wigs
       and sofas
          and teevee sets —

Running
      after
        the merchandise
All the
      commercials
        advertise

on teevee
on teevee
on teevee...

VOL

I Had a Little

I had a little teevee,
Kept it over there,
Over by the window;
Now the place is bare.

The installment collector
Came to visit me,
And all for the sake of
My little teevee.

Hushabye Baby

Hushabye, baby,
On the top floor,
Project elevator
Won't work anymore.

It comes up to ten
And then starts to stall;
We'll have to walk down, baby,
Carriage and all.

Hickory Dickory Dock

Hickory dickory dock,
The crowd ran up the block.

A cop struck one,
A rock got thrown;
Hickory dickory riot.

This Little Pig

This little pig on the corner,
This little pig in the car,
This little pig in plain clothes,
This little pig with a star,
And this little pig cried We-we-we-we-we
Want Wallace.

Tom, Tom

Tom, Tom,
Uncle Tom's son;

It's getting hard
To find one.

No more mild and meek   No more fetch and tote   Not now.
And turn the other cheek,   No more scrape and bow.   Not Now.   NOT NOW.

Run, Run

Run, run father, go away:
Welfare worker is due today.

One, Two

One, two,
Welfare for you;

Three, four,
Agency door;

Five, six,
Caseworker picks;

Seven, eight,
Investigate;

Nine, ten,
Fill out more forms
and wait in line all over again.

One, two,
Welfare for you;

Three, four,
Agency door;

Five, six,
Caseworker picks;

Seven, eight,
Investigate;

Nine, ten,
Fill out more forms
and wait in line all over again.

One, two,
Welfare for you;

Three, four,
Agency door;

Five, six,
Caseworker picks;

Seven, eight,
Investigate;

Nine, ten,
Fill out more forms
and wait in line all over again.

One, two,
Welfare for you;

Three, four,
Agency door;

Five, six,
Caseworker picks;

Seven, eight,
Investigate;

Nine, ten,
Fill out more forms
and wait in line all over again.

One, two,
Welfare for you;

Three, four,
Agency door;

Five, six,
Caseworker picks;

Seven, eight,
Investigate;

Nine, ten,
Fill out more forms
and wait in line all over again.

One, two,
Welfare for you;

Three, four,
Agency door;

Five, six,
Caseworker picks;

Seven, eight,
Investigate;

Nine, ten,
Fill out more forms
and wait in line all over again.

One, two,
Welfare for you;

Three, four,
Agency door;

Five, six,
Caseworker picks;

Seven, eight,
Investigate;

One Misty Moisty Morning

One misty moisty morning,
Virus was the weather;
Waiting for the bus to come,
Closed in together.

One began to cough and shake,
Another cursed his mother,
Someone swiped a wallet:
A day like any other.

Twelve Rooftops Leaping

12 rooftops leaping
11 windows smashing
10 pipes abursting
9 sirens screaming
8 phone booths broken
7 bulbs adimming
6 junkies trading
5 stolen rings
4 padlocked stores
3 slashed tires
2 cherry bombs

And a scout group planting a tree.

As I Went Over

As I went over the precinct,
A rage swept over me.
I saw two little black boys
Scooting around free.
One called me a honky
And one called me a thief,
I took up my little nightstick
And knocked out all their teeth.

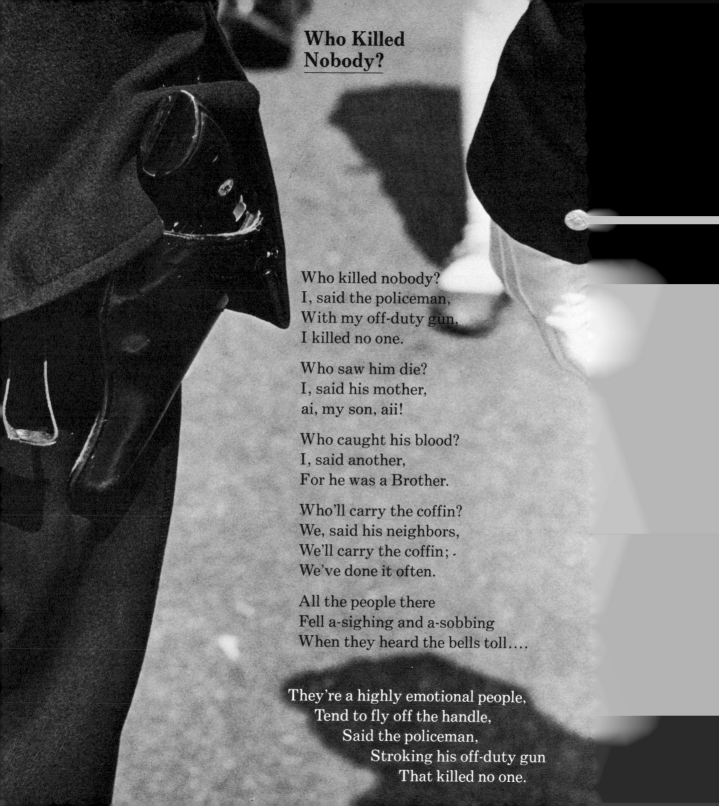

Who Killed
Nobody?

Who killed nobody?
I, said the policeman,
With my off-duty gun,
I killed no one.

Who saw him die?
I, said his mother,
ai, my son, aii!

Who caught his blood?
I, said another,
For he was a Brother.

Who'll carry the coffin?
We, said his neighbors,
We'll carry the coffin; .
We've done it often.

All the people there
Fell a-sighing and a-sobbing
When they heard the bells toll....

They're a highly emotional people,
Tend to fly off the handle,
Said the policeman,
Stroking his off-duty gun
That killed no one.

Fee, Fi, Fo, Fum

Fee, fi, fo, fum, I smell the blood of violence to come; I smell the smoke that hangs in the air

Of buildings burning everywhere; Even the rats abandon the city: The situation is being studied
by a crisis committee.

There Was a Man

There was a man of our town
And he was wondrous wise—

He moved away.

The ailing heart of American cities
has been the subject of many books—
but none more telling,
none more jarring,
than this gathering of
nursery rhymes, altered
from their classic form
to dramatize the desperation
of life in our urban ghettos.
Never has innocence been put
to more potent social use than in
The Inner City Mother Goose.